ICE CREAM LARRY

Daniel Pinkwater

Illustrated by
Jill Pinkwater

MARSHALL CAVENDISH • NEW YORK

"HELLO?"

"We have your bear."

"Oh my! Where is he?"

"He is at Cohen's Cones, the ice-cream shop. He will not leave. Someone will have to come and take him away."

I could hear Larry saying, "I think I will have another blueberry sundae."

"No! No more!" I heard someone say.

Larry is a polar bear. He lives in our hotel. Once, Larry saved my father's life, and that is why the hotel is called the Hotel Larry. Larry is the lifeguard at the hotel pool.

I hurried down to the ice-cream shop.

Mrs. Cohen was the owner of Cohen's Cones.

"Out of the goodness of my heart, I allowed this bear to sleep in the walk-in freezer. Now, I find he has eaten over two hundred and fifty pounds of ice cream."

I looked at Larry.

"Please don't worry about me. I feel fine," Larry said.

"Why did you let him sleep in your freezer?" I asked Mrs. Cohen.

"He said he was warm."

"Didn't you think he might eat the ice cream?" I asked.

"He said we had nothing to fear," Mrs. Cohen said.

"I think he meant to tell you that he would not eat any people," I said. "He won't, you know."

"Eat people?"

"That's right."

"I don't see how you can let a bear into your freezer and not expect him to eat ice cream," I said.

"He ate a lot," Mrs. Cohen said.

"Well, he's a bear."

"I suppose."

"I didn't eat any of the almond crunch," Larry said. "Could I have some now please?"

"No," said Mrs. Cohen.

"My father will pay for the ice cream," I said. "Larry is his very best friend."

"In that case, you may each have an almond crunch cone," Mrs. Cohen said. "But take the bear away."

Larry and I walked away from Cohen's Cones, licking our almond crunches.

"It was wrong to eat all that ice cream," I said.

"I became overheated," Larry said. "I only intended to have a nap. I think I ate the ice cream in my sleep."

"You continued asking for ice cream when you were awake," I said.

"Well, yes," Larry said. "I saw no harm in it. The customers seemed to think it was cute, and a man came in and took my picture."

The next day, Larry's picture was in the newspaper.

"Bear eats eighth of a ton of ice cream," it said above the picture.

Under the picture, it said, "'I do not feel sick,' says bear."

"Mildred, you know Larry is not supposed to leave the hotel without you," my father said.

"Mildred was at her karate lesson," Larry said. "I became bored."

"I have paid for the ice cream. We will say no more about it," my father said.

A man came to stay at the hotel. He signed his name in the book at the desk: I. BERG.

"This is the hotel where the polar bear lives, is it not?" I. Berg asked.

"Oh, yes," my mother said.

"May I see him?" I. Berg asked.

"He is sleeping. He ate a great deal of ice cream yesterday," my mother said. "But I am sure you will see him later."

After supper, Mr. Berg approached my father. He gave my father a card that read

I. BERG

ICEBERG ICE-CREAM COMPANY

"Are you the bear's owner?" Mr. Berg asked my father.

"Owner? No. He is my friend," my father said.

"Would it be possible for me to speak to him on a matter of business?"

"He is a wild polar bear and may speak to whomever he likes. But I would like to be present."

"Of course," said Mr. I. Berg.

Larry and my father and Mr. Berg sat together in the lobby.

"It is my honor to own the Iceberg Ice-Cream Company, of Baltimore, Maryland, founded in 1851. You may know our slogan, 'Iceberg! Iceberg! We all scream for Iceberg!'"

"I'm not sure I understand it," Larry said.

"No," Mr. Berg said. "No one seems to."

"Still, it's a catchy slogan," my father said.

"Larry, your picture has been copied in newspapers all over the world. People know that you ate a half ton of ice cream at Cohen's Cones, but they do not know that it was Iceberg ice cream you ate."

"It was only an eighth of a ton," Larry said.

"Still, it was a lot of ice cream," Mr. Berg said.

"I was overheated and hungry," Larry said. "I am often hungry."

"I had to pay for all of it," my father said.

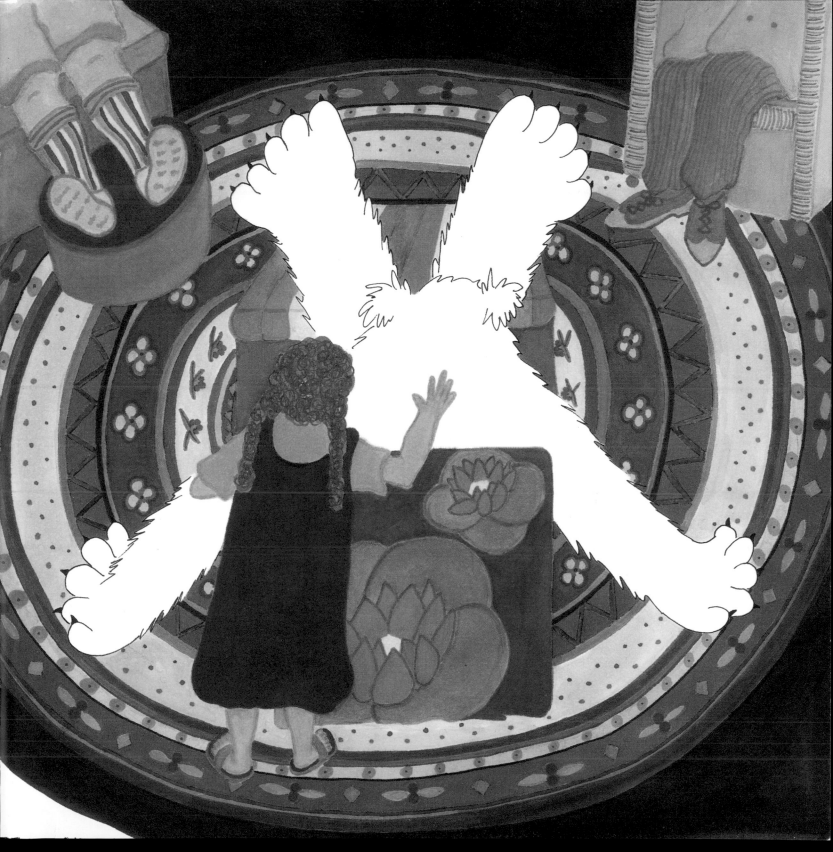

"Larry, would you like to come with me to Baltimore, Maryland? I can show you our modern ice-cream factory. I will bring you home the very next day."

"Mr. Berg, I think I would like to go to Baltimore, Maryland, visit a modern ice-cream factory, and come home the very next day more than anything else I can imagine at this moment," Larry said.

In the morning, Larry and Mr. Berg went away in a very large car. Larry wore his sunglasses. He took with him a small suitcase containing his bongos and a paperback copy of *Moby Dick* by Herman Melville.

The following day, Mr. Berg brought Larry back to the hotel.

"Did you have a nice time in Baltimore, Maryland?" I asked Larry.

"I had a very nice time," Larry said.

"Was the modern ice-cream factory interesting?" I asked.

"Yes. It was quite modern, and very interesting. I learned a great deal," Larry said.

"Why did Mr. Berg want to show it to you, and what did you learn, and what did you do?" I asked.

"I would prefer to tell you about it at another time," Larry said.

"You won't tell me now?"

"I would prefer not to."

Larry continued to refuse to talk about his visit to Baltimore, Maryland. He said nothing to my father and nothing to my mother and nothing to me.

Mr. Berg visited Larry a number of times. Larry would sit in the very large car with Mr. Berg, and they would look at sheets of paper and talk to each other.

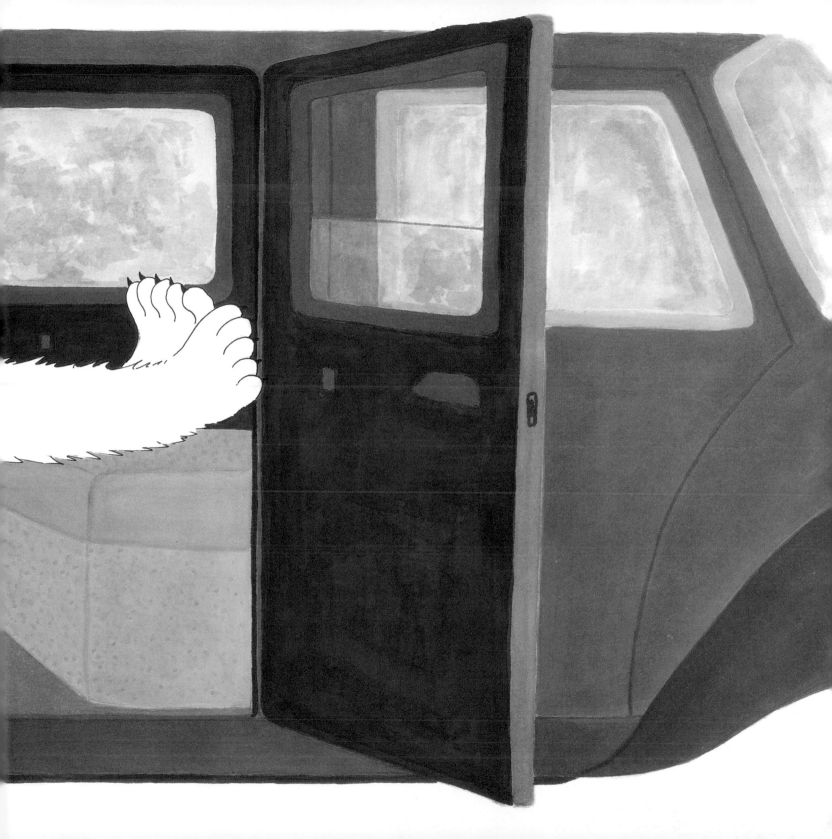

One day, Mr. Berg brought a very large box made of plastic foam. He dragged it into the hotel, then called us to gather around.

"Behold!" Mr. Berg said. He took the lid off the box. It was full of ice-cream bars, each with a picture of Larry on the wrapper.

"I give you the Larry Bar!" Mr. Berg said.

"I am so proud," Larry said.

The Larry Bars came in many flavors: vanilla, chocolate, strawberry, blueberry and arctic almond, bearberry, polar pineapple, and codfish.

"The codfish was my idea," Larry said. "Mr. Berg is not too sure about that one, but I know it will be popular."

Mr. Berg unrolled a large poster. It had a picture of
Larry holding all the flavors of Larry Bars in his paws.
At the top it said

THE LARRY BAR

and at the bottom, it said

I DO NOT FEEL SICK!

"Our new slogan!" Mr. Berg said.

The rest is history. Larry Bars are loved by everyone, and the codfish flavor Larry Bar is considered a gourmet treat.

There are posters, signs, and billboards of Larry, and the slogan "I do not feel sick" is known the world over.

Larry has appeared on television, and he received a phone call from the President of the United States. He is a celebrity. He is the spokesbear for the Iceberg Ice-Cream Company.

I asked Larry, "Does Mr. Berg pay you anything for helping to make Larry Bars famous?"

"I did not come all the way from Baffin Bay to be a fool," Larry said. "Have you seen the new walk-in freezer in my room? What is more, I receive fifty Larry Bars each day."

"It sounds like a good deal to me," I said.

"Oh, yes. I am a happy bear," Larry said.

Thanks to Samuel's of Rhinebeck, New York,
where we thought up this book.

Marshall Cavendish, 99 White Plains Road, Tarrytown, New York 10591
The text of this book is set in 16 point Esprit Book
The illustrations are rendered in pen and ink and colored markers
Printed in Italy
First edition

Library of Congress Cataloging-in-Publication Data. Pinkwater, Daniel Manus
Ice-cream Larry / by Daniel Pinkwater ; illustrated by Jill Pinkwater.   p.   cm. Summary: After he eats an
eighth of a ton of ice cream at Cohen's Cones, Larry the polar bear happily becomes the spokesbear for the Iceberg
Ice-Cream Company under the slogan, "I do not feel sick." ISBN 0-7614-5043-2
[1. Polar bear — Fiction. 2. Bears — Fiction. 3. Ice Cream, ices, etc. — Fiction. 4. Humorous stories.]
I. Pinkwater, Jill, ill. II. Title.
PZ7.P6335Ig 1999   [Fic]—dc21   98-8832   CIP   AC

E
Pin

Pinkwater, Daniel
Ice Cream Larry

This book donated to
First Grade Jewish Studies
from The Heskes Family

January 2004